T0130564

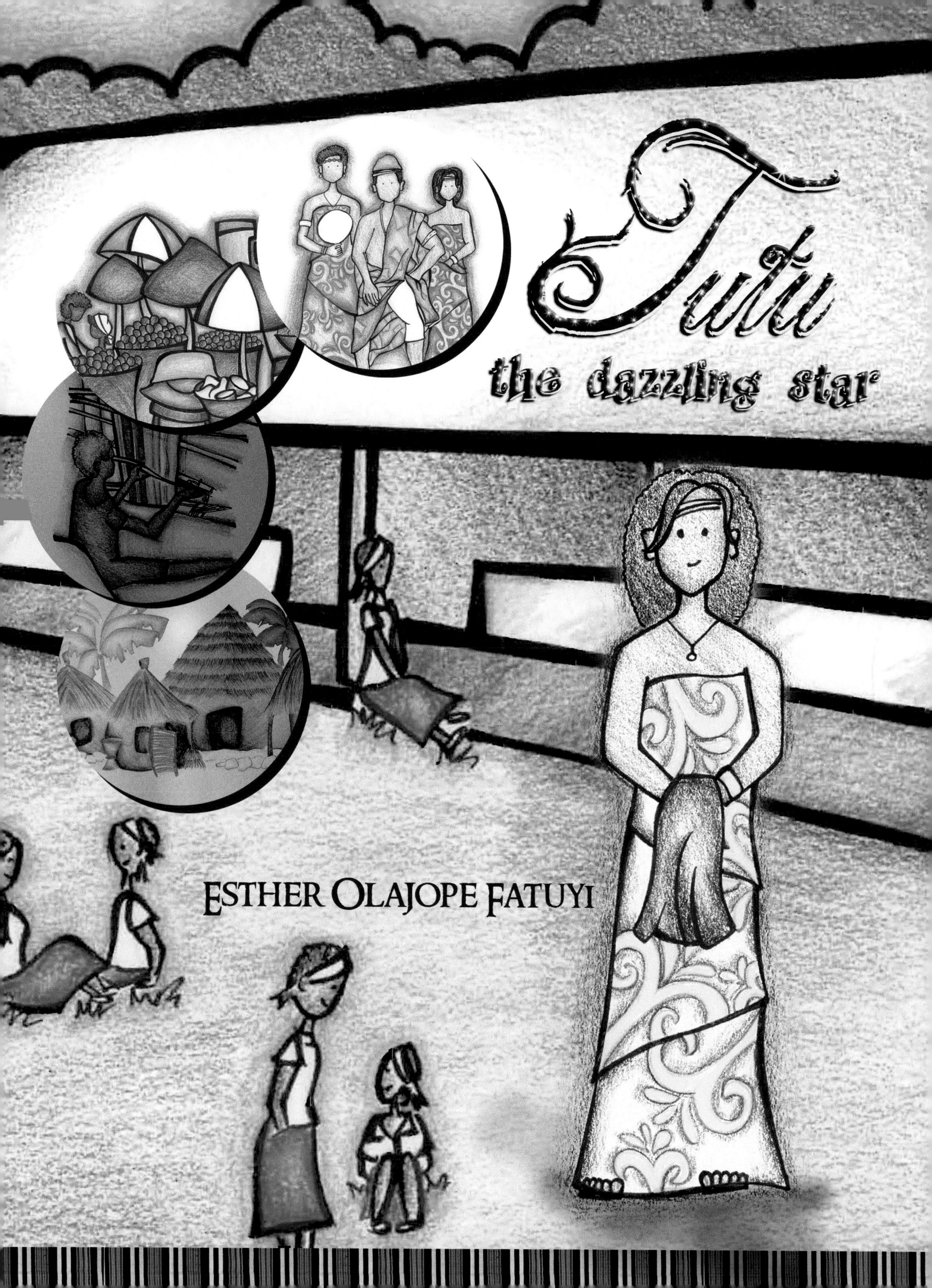
Tutu
the dazzling star
ESTHER OLAJOPE FATUYI

This is a work of fiction. Names, characters, places and incidents either are the product of the author's imagination or are used fictitiously, and any resemblance to any actual persons, living or dead, events, or locales is entirely coincidental.

To order additional copies of this book, contact:
Xlibris
844-714-8691
www.Xlibris.com
Orders@Xlibris.com

ISBN:	Softcover	978-1-6641-8249-3
	Hardcover	978-1-6641-8250-9
	EBook	978-1-6641-8248-6

Print information available on the last page

Rev. date: 07/21/2021

To the Almighty who is able
be all the glory, honor, majesty, and dominion.

I want to bring attention first and foremost to my mother, Eunice Adetutu Akomolafe, for telling me the story that soon went on to become this book. I am also grateful for the help of Linda Moore, the executive director of Elsie Whitlow Stokes Public Charter School, Washington DC, for giving me the opportunity to become the first professional Library and Media Specialist at the school. The experience gave me insight into the fundamentals of reading and the importance of instilling that at the core of children to make them lifelong learners; it also gave me the opportunity to identify the reading needs and gaps to be filled in the education of children.

I want to appreciate Dr. Remi Tokunbo Okwechime for her insight and contributions toward the successful completion of the manuscript. I also appreciate Barrister Ayodeji Wande Aire for her critical contributions to this revised edition. I thank Tony Okwechime, Ehimare Aire and my granddaughter Fiyinfoluwa Oluwatitomi Okwechime who read through the manuscript for their constructive comments. I thank Chief Isaac Akomolafe, Mofe Akomolafe, Funbi Ajuwon, Akin Ajuwon, Dr. Remi Fatuyi, Barrister Yewande Fatuyi, Bimpe Anthony-Wise and my grandchildren for supporting me, believing in me, and cheering me on to complete this revised edition of the book.

I have to recognize the hard working Cloth Weavers in the environment where this author was raised. Some of their creativity in woven clothes are displayed on the pages of this book.

Chapter One

HARD WORK DOES NOT KILL BUT LAZINESS DOES

Tutu was born in a peaceful village to the village pastor and his petty trader wife. She lived with her parents and older brothers in this typical African village.

Tutu was the last child and the only surviving daughter of her mother. Her older siblings adored her and treated her like a Princess. Although she was pampered and well loved, little Tutu was quite the entrepreneur. She always had a new idea or scheme to get things done. Tutu strived to be above the leisurely life her parents and older siblings wanted her to have . Her parents didn't allow her to begin school at the conventional time because they feared that she might be mistreated or bullied if she started school too early.

They therefore decided to train her at home and expose her to trading until she was old enough to cope with harder chores and able to handle other responsibilities at home.

Tutu's mother taught her to sew. She learned the art of sewing quickly and she would constantly practice what she had learned by sewing for her dolls. She was making her own clothes in no time.

* * *

One rainy day, Tutu's older brother came back from school in his wet clothes. Tutu was curious about her brother's day at school and why he was not cold in spite of the heavy rain.

Her brother showed her his school uniform, and Tutu exclaimed that the uniform was thicker than the usual fabric often used, heavy and not very wet. Her brother explained to her that their mother bought the material from a neighbor who weaves with a loom and then sewed it into a school uniform. Excited,, she begged her parents to let her learn weaving from their neighbor. "Please, Father?" Tutu said, her eyes darting between him and Mother. "Think of all the good it would do to me. I'd be learning a new skill. A helpful one."

Her father only shook his head. "I don't know, Tutu. Do you have the time for it?"

The only thing that she could do now was ask Mother. Tutu turned to her with wide eyes. "You learned to weave when you were my age, Mother? Please, give me a chance."

"Alright," her mother said, she looked at Tutu's father and continued. "I think we should give her a chance and since it's going to be with our neighbor, we could still keep her under our watchful eyes while keeping her occupied when she's not doing her chores."

Turning to Tutu, she said "Do you think you can handle this new skill along with your chores?"

"Yes yes, Mother Tutu said, "I will do perfectly well, please, give me the chance to show you what I am capable of doing, I promise not to disappoint both of you."

Her father replied, "As long as you promise to do a good job in your daily chores and the training skill of weaving, you have our blessings. We will sign you up with our neighbor."

"Oh thank you Father, thank you both so much!

* * *

TUTU LEARNS A TRADE

Tutu went with her parents to ask their neighbor to teach her to weave. The woman had always been impressed with Tutu's good manners. She was delighted to have Tutu learn to weave on the loom, and she accepted her as an apprentice. Tutu would run errands for her in order to pay for her weaving lessons. .

* * *

Tutu learned the art of weaving on the loom under the tutelage of their neighbor for two years, and when she had become proficient, she celebrated her "freedom"—a ceremony involving an apprentice presenting gifts to a tutor at the successful completion of an apprenticeship. She presented five tubers of yam, a keg of the local wine, a bowl of kola nuts, a bottle of organic honey, and a bowl of bitter kola to her tutor as a symbol of her final release and freedom.

Tutu was now adept at the art of weaving and soon started selling her clothes to mothers who would sew the woven clothes into school uniforms for their children. They also sewed the woven clothes into work clothes for their husbands and wards in the village. The village women admired little Tutu because of her diligence and allowed no room for incompetence.

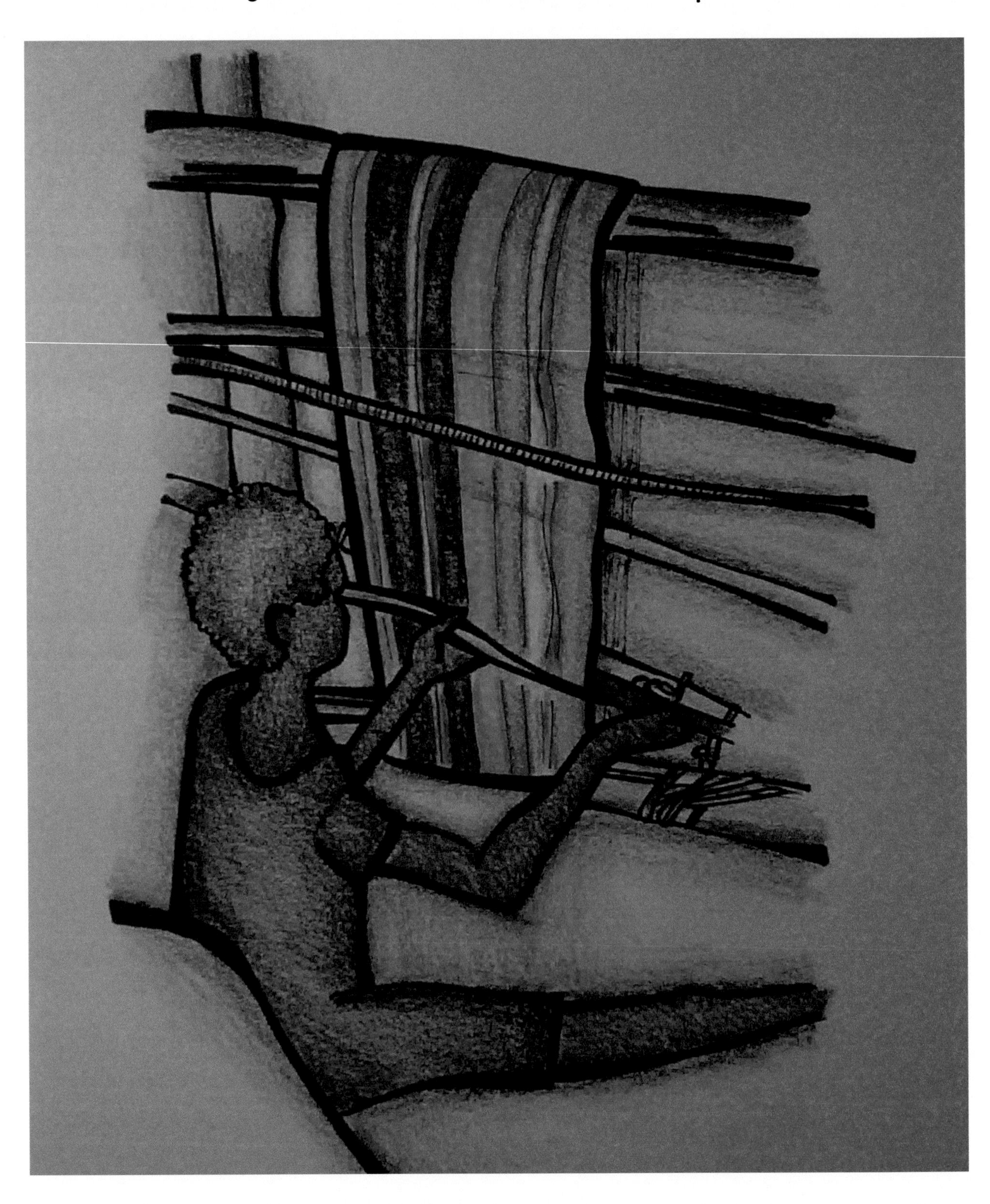

Tutu sold her woven clothes to the farmers at the village market every ninth day. The farmers usually brought their produce to the market every market day for sale. After selling their produce, they would spend some of the proceeds from their chores. The farmers became regular customers of Tutu because she was very creative, and her colorful clothes were highly sought after by her customers. She maintained high standards for her woven clothes because she believed that "*things worth doing at all are worth doing well, things done by half are never done well.*" Word reached the nearby villages, and they also came to her village to buy her woven clothes for work and uniforms for their children.

On a cold evening, Tutu's grandmother took her to see her friend, who was an old widow. The old woman, who was with two other old women, was telling stories and drinking hot herbal soup to keep warm.

Tutu had compassion for these elderly village women and promised to weave thicker clothes for them. Tutu made good on her promise by weaving the clothes and getting the clothes to the women before the next ninth village market day. The elderly women expressed their appreciation and admiration for Tutu. They prayed for her success in life and sent a message to the village chief to let him know, according to the village custom. A villager had shown great kindness to the elderly and set an example.

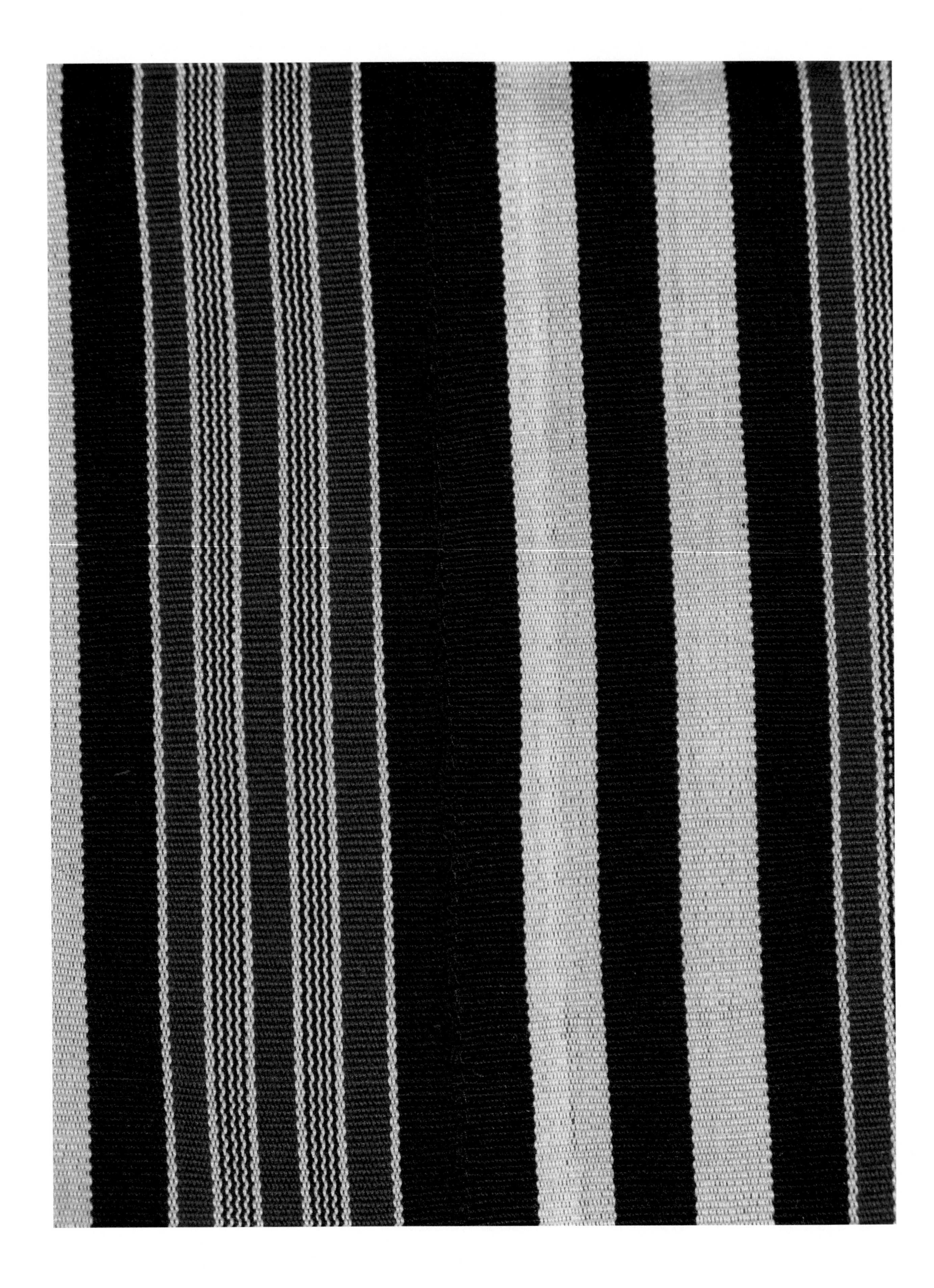

Tutu worked so hard that, soon afterwards, she had many more orders of woven clothes than she could sell in her small village. She considered taking her woven clothes to a bigger village nearby because she would have more customers there. The weekly market day at the bigger village took place every five days, and many farmers, from various farms would come to sell their produce and to buy various items. Tutu asked her mother and her aunt if they would go with her to the bigger village, and they agreed to go with her. They were excited and determined to encourage her hard work.

* * *

At dawn on the market day, Tutu was already up! She woke up her mother and her aunt to start their long trek to the big market. The market was two-hour walk from Tutu's village. They met other women on the way to the market, and they exchanged greetings and asked after each other's families as was the custom of the people. One woman who joined the travelers from another village commented that "it takes a hardworking individual to make such a long trip from the village to the big market."

She went on to inform the travelers that she was not able to come to the market on the previous market day because of an incident that happened in their village. Tutu's mother and aunt asked what happened, and the woman told them that there was a village gathering at the center of her village, and the chief of that village announced that a ten-year-old orphan needed help to pay for his school. The village chief made an announcement that the entire village should come together to contribute, in cash or kind, to assist this orphan. Tutu was immediately interested in helping this boy even though his village was a twenty-minute walk from Tutu's village.

The long trip to the big market was usually made by members of the smaller villages around, with the items for sale carried on their heads and sometimes with their babies carried on their backs.

Tutu, her mother, and her aunt arrived at the big village market at the same time that other traders were arriving. They stopped by the well at the entrance to the market to wash their legs and to remove the dust that had gathered from walking such a long distance. The travelers, however, did not show any signs of weariness because they were excited and enthusiastic to see what the day would bring in terms of Tutu's trade in her first big-market experience.

* * *

Tutu was very excited to set up and display her beautiful clothes, which she had carefully selected with her mother and aunt's help. She selected a good central spot in the market for the display of her woven clothes. She was full of expectation and anticipated good sales because she had worked hard on weaving the clothes and had used beautiful colors very creatively.

Tutu's mother and aunt helped her to display the woven clothes on strong strings attached to two poles on each side of the market stall. It was a beautiful and colorful display.

Tutu had used dye made of local plants and herbs to color the wool before weaving the cloths on the loom. The process of making the dye and applying it to the wool drew many villagers' attention to Tutu's creativity.

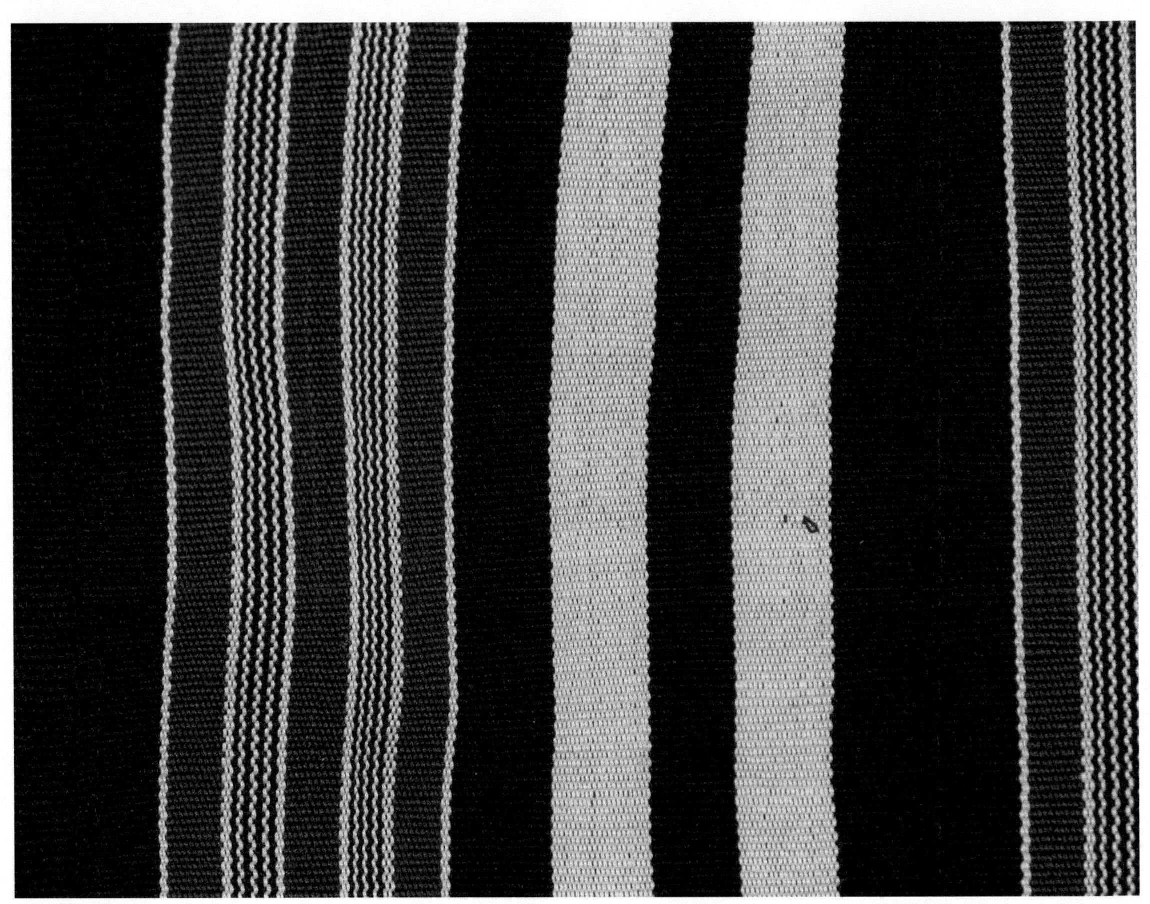

By midday, Tutu had practically finished selling her woven clothes. The local farmers came in droves to Tutu's stall to buy woven clothes as soon as they had sold off their farm produce. They made their selection from the woven collection of clothes Tutu had on display.

She had something for everyone! The farmers left her stall happy and content with their purchases.

By the time the last farmer left Tutu's stall, her mother and her aunt, who had been going about their own chores, returned to help Tutu pack up. To their amazement, there were absolutely no clothes left. Every single one had been sold!

They exclaimed in unison, "Where are the woven clothes?"

"Sold out," replied Tutu with a huge and contented grin on her face. All her work had paid off. Her mother and her aunt gave her big hugs, and packed up the food items that they bought and hurried back to their village before dark, singing on their way as they journeyed.

"Hard work is the right medicine. The right medicine and the cure for poverty." As they journeyed on, Tutu saw a bird in the front, struggling to hop. Upon closer look, she discovered that the bird is a parrot that has been wounded and struggling to move. Tutu had compassion on the bird and convinced her mum and aunt that she would like to keep the bird and nurse it back to health. The adults agreed with her saying that she has a kind heart and in unison they said that the bird is a good omen. Tutu picked up the bird, named him Dinke and they continued on their journey home.

Since they had a lot less to carry, the trio was able to travel faster and arrived at their village on time for the family's evening meal. The entire family gathered excitedly in anticipation of sharing Tutu's experience of her first big market encounter. They were pleasantly surprised when Tutu informed them about how successful she had been on her first big market day and excitedly showed the family the parrot that she found on her way back.

"You sold all your woven clothes?" asked a great aunt; Tutu's grandmother held her tightly on her lap and told her she was very proud of her and commented that the parrot is also a good omen. The celebration continued when Tutu's great aunt came in with a big bowl of pounded yam (iyan) with (egusi) soup for the entire family. They had a huge feast!

Afterwards, Grandma Ote reminded everyone about the saying of the elders which was the family motto, and had been passed on from generation to generation in the village... "hard work does not kill, but laziness does." Tutu told everyone about her experience on the way to the market. She said that she had made up her mind to contribute some of her earnings to help the orphan from the nearby village get an education. Her grandmother offered to accompany her to see the chief of their village so they could inform him of their plans. The chief would select a messenger from the palace to go with Tutu to see the chief of the next village and to make the donation. Tutu took two of her woven clothes as a present for both her village chief and the chief of the next village. She also took an extra woven cloth to make a school uniform for the orphan boy.

* * *

On the next market day, the chief of Tutu's village sent her off to the chief of the next village in company of the messenger. The village chief announced this good deed of Tutu to the entire village and declared that Tutu had done a great thing to make the village proud and encouraged the other villagers to also assist the orphan.

* * *

Chapter Two

A LISTENING EAR IS OF GREAT VALUE

On a cold November morning, Tutu's brother, Dami, came home with a sniffle. "Oh dear," his mother said. "Put on some warm clothes and sit by the fire. Come, I will make you some tea." She made some herbal tea, from a recipe that was used by many of the villagers for colds and flu. "Okay, Mum. I will do just that". His clothes got wet because he stopped to play in the stream on the way home from school, he said. But as he went to his room, he saw Tutu making dinner in the kitchen.

"What are you cooking for dinner?" he asked.

"Plantain porridge," she replied. "Your clothes are so wet! Why don't you change them and put on some dry clothes? You can get sick, you know."

"Shh, Mum will hear you. I'm trying to escape from her. She wants to give me her famous herbal tea and it's so bitter! On the other hand, what you're cooking Smells delicious!" Dami said as he licked his lips. "They are my favorite. I'd rather sit down here and treat myself to some of that yummy food." He sat down right there in the kitchen and began to dig into the meal.

"I wouldn't do that if I were you," Tutu said. "I know it's bitter, but it does help treat a cold."

"Hmpff!" Dami scoffed. "What do you know? I'll do as I please."

"Okay, brother, suit yourself. After all, it's up to you. Whatever actions you take are yours and yours alone," Tutu said sweetly.

"You got that right!" Dami replied with a smile.

He forgot to change his wet clothes; he did not take his tea and did not sit by the fire. By the time he was done eating, he was too full to go back into the living room, and he stumbled into his room and fell asleep right away. By this time, his clothes had dried up while still on him, and he slept in them.

* * *

The next morning, Dami felt like an elephant was sitting on his chest. It was difficult to breathe. He started coughing really badly, and it felt like someone had turned the heat up in his room. It was so hot!

As he tried to get out of bed, he noticed his chest was aching, and he was in a lot of pain. His mum walked in.

"Dami, you are late for school! What happened? Did you just wake up?" "Mum, I don't feel too good," he replied.

She put her hand on his forehead. "It looks like you have a fever! Did you sleep in wet clothes?"

A sheepish-looking Dami nodded.

"Did you drink the herbal tea I made for you and did you sit by the fire?" his mum asked.

"No, Mum, I'm afraid I didn't. I didn't want to drink that herbal tea because it's bitter. I'm sorry, Mum, I forgot to change my clothes and I also didn't sit by the fire," Dami replied in a small voice.

"Well, I told you what to do, and you wouldn't listen or obey. See the consequences? You've got the flu!"

She hurried him over to the village doctor who confirmed their worst fears and said he had pneumonia, which was even worse than the flu. He had to rest at home for many days with Tutu taking care of him.

“I’ll never disobey Mum again. If I had only listened to Mother, I wouldn’t be in this situation.” he sobbed. “Don’t you worry. I’ll be here to take care of you,” Tutu said enthusiastically.

“But I’m in a lot of pain!” Dami exclaimed.

“Well, what can I say? A listening ear is of great value! If you had listened to Mum and I, you wouldn’t be sick now.”

“I agree with you. It pays to listen and to be obedient,” a repentant Dami acknowledged. “Thanks for your advice and help. I appreciate it.”

“Not a problem. What are sisters for?” Tutu said as they both laughed it off.

* * *

Chapter Three

A REWARD FOR A GOOD HEART

A few years later, on a bright sunny day, Tutu was going to the stream to fetch water for her family. Along the way, she met an old pauper who asked her to help him to the stream since he needed water to drink.

Tutu felt sorry for the man and was happy to help. "Oh, not a problem, sir!" she said. Tutu helped him to the stream and even gave him water to drink from her pitcher.

Unknown to Tutu, this was the king of the next town in disguise! He was in disguise to look for a bride for his son. He wanted to choose a well-bred lady with a good heart who would love his son not because he was rich, but for himself. The king had been doing this for days, waiting for the right lady to come along since his son was of age to be married and he, the king, was to retire. The king was glad that he had finally found someone with a kind heart. He asked her for her name, and Tutu told him. "What a lovely name!" the king told Tutu. At this point, the king had not revealed himself to her, so she still thought he was an old pauper. He gave her a gold coin and thanked her for her kindness.

Tutu then fetched her water and went on her way.

* * *

Meanwhile, the king decided to stay a little longer at the stream to see if anyone else would come by. A little while after this, another lady from Tutu's village walked by on her way to the stream. Her name was Clara. Clara was a spoiled child. She never did as she was told, and she was often rude to her parents. Not only would she be rude to them but to outsiders as well. She was asked by her mother to fetch water early in the morning on that day, but she took her time and was strolling to the stream an hour later. She also saw the old pauper but walked as far away from him as possible.

"Hello, my child," he called to her. "Please can you help me to the stream since I've come on a long journey, and I'm so thirsty?"

"What?" she said. "Who is your child? I can never be the child of an old, dirty man like you! Help yourself to the stream. At least you have legs to walk!" And with that, she stormed off to fetch her water, mumbling under her breath. "Who does he think he is calling his child..."

The king decided to give her another chance. He hobbled to the stream and got there just as Clara was about to lift her pitcher to her head. "Please can I get a little to drink from your pitcher?" he asked her politely.

"No, you may not! It's bad enough that I'm speaking with you, I don't want to contaminate my water pitcher with the germs from your mouth!" Clara laughed sarcastically and walked off.

"Hold on," he said. "I just want to give you a little gift." She stopped and looked at him. He held a gold coin in his hand. "Well, if you must, okay." She took it from him without even saying thank you and went back to the village.

The king decided he had had enough of his disguise and went back to his kingdom.

* * *

A little while later, he sent for his most trusted adviser and told him to go to the next village and summon all the eligible young ladies to the village hall and ask for whoever was given a gold coin by an old pauper by the stream during the past month to come forward and show him the coin.

There was a particular gold coin that had the signet ring of the king imprinted on it, and that was what he was to look out for. He was to single out the lady who had it and give her the gifts he brought. The king told him to take with him gifts fit for a Princess. He told him to saddle ten camels with food, robes, jewelry, and wine as gifts for the family of the girl. He also told him not to tell the girl that she was going to marry a Prince. Since he had been going to that stream for about a month, he assumed that he had met all the young eligible ladies who were of marriageable age in the neighboring village, so he could confidently say his search for a bride for his son was over.

* * *

The next day, the king's chief adviser took servants with him and the ten camels laden with food, jewelry, clothes, and wine along to the next village. He then went to the village market center and announced his intentions to the villagers who had gathered.

The village people sent for their daughters and asked who was given a gold coin. Tutu was home when her mother came running.

Her mother had gone to see her friend when she heard the news. "My dear child, I remember you came home one day with a gold coin. There is a stranger in the village center with gifts for the lady who has a particular gold coin. Let's go back there to see if it's the same coin and find out what it is that they are looking for." Tutu's mum blurted out in excitement.

Tutu hurriedly got the coin, and together with her mum, they ran back to the village market center.

* * *

On the other side of the village, Clara's mum was kneading flour outside her house when she heard people spreading the news about the stranger in the village market center and his gifts. She moved closer to hear what they were saying.

Clara was playing skip rope in front of their hut and stopped to listen also. "Oh, Mother!" she cried out. "I was given an old coin a few days ago!"

"Is that so?" her mother asked. "But you told me nothing of the sort. Let me see this gold coin. I have always told you to show me anything given to you by a stranger, but you never listen."

Clara sheepishly ran to her room at the back of the hut and brought out the gold coin from underneath her bed. It was covered in dust; apparently, she hadn't even cleaned her room in days. "It's so dusty!" her mother exclaimed. "Did you sweep your room? When did you last have it dusted?" Clara looked away ashamed. "I'm sorry, Mum," she muttered, insincerely.

"Come on. Let's go to the town hall and see if your gold coin is the one they are looking for!" Clara's mum pulled her sixteen-year-old daughter's hand, and they ran to the village center.

They were just in time because the chief advisor to the king was making his last announcement and beginning to inspect all the gold coins brought by the eligible ladies of the village. When it got to Clara's turn, she was so sure hers was the coin they were looking for and was highly disappointed when the man inspected it and shook his head. "It can't be," she shouted. "It has to be mine!"

"Please be calm," he told her. "Everybody gets a turn."

Tutu was next in line. As he inspected hers, his face lit up with a smile. "Here it is! The signet ring of the king is imprinted on it."

* * *

"Congratulations, for you have earned these gifts due to your kind heart. You were the only one who was nice to an old pauper who sat by the wayside on the way to the village stream, and you helped him to the stream and even offered him water to drink. Listen everyone and learn from this, it pays to be nice!" he commented. And with that, he called the servants with the camels and offered the gifts to Tutu and her mother. Tutu was overjoyed and so was her mother. They hugged each other with tears running down their cheeks. "Thank you so much," they said in unison.

"No, I should be the one saying thank you for training your daughter well," the chief adviser told her. "Now as for the rest of you who were too proud to help an old man, we will offer to send you to a training school for young ladies, between the ages of sixteen and eighteen years, a few miles from here to teach you how to behave and to be well-bred," he declared and prepared to enroll those interested in the proposed school before leaving the village market center.

Clara's mum was so angry with her daughter. "You mean you weren't nice to the old pauper? How many times have I told you to be nice and help others and lend a helping hand? You see what it has cost you? You would have won these lovely gifts, and you know how much we need them. I'm going to send you to that school, and I hope they teach you a lesson there!"

"Please, Mum, don't send me away from home. How would I survive without you and Daddy? Oh no." She sobbed.

The other mothers with their children at the village center scolded their girls and began enrolling them at the school. There was even a wait list.

Tutu's mum looked at her daughter. "Today, you have made me so proud, my child. What do you say? Would you like to also go to the school?"

“No knowledge is lost, Mother, so why not? Yes, I would love to,” she said with a smile. “Okay then, let’s enroll you,” Tutu’s mum replied.

So Tutu was enrolled in the school to start a couple of months later. She would miss her family and “Dinke” the parrot that she had nursed to health and to whom she is now very close. Her mother promised to look after the parrot.

* * *

Chapter Four

TUTU GOES TO SCHOOL

It was the first day of school. Everyone was excited because the school was the first of its kind in the big town. It was a school that taught ladies how to work to provide for the family as well as to cook, clean, and keep the house. It also taught them good morals. They were each given two pairs of uniforms and two pairs of sweatshirts and pants for sports activities in their physical education class.

Tutu was shown to her hall by the School Warden. A few hours later, the students all assembled for the evening gatherings in the school hall.

The School Mistress had a big announcement to make. "Here are the rules for each weekday. You are to wake up at 5:30 a.m., go for your morning workout, and come back to take your shower at 6:00 a.m. At 6:30 a.m., you will clean your surroundings, and at 6:45 a.m everyday, there will be an inspection of your beds and uniforms. At 7:00 a.m, you will all have breakfast. At 7:30 a.m., you should go back to your hostels and take your books to class. Classes begin at 8:00 a.m. prompt. No lateness will be tolerated. Is that understood?"

Everybody nodded. "Okay then, lunch break is between 11:30 a.m. and 1:00 p.m. Lectures end at 3:00 p.m., afternoon prep is at 4:00 p.m., dinner is at 6:00 p.m. Evening prep will be at 7:00 p.m. Lights-out will be at 9:00 p.m., and I will not tolerate anyone sneaking out of their hostels for anything after lights- out!" she warned.

Clara was standing far away at the back of the crowd of students. "No way am I waking up at 5:30 a.m.!" she complained. "Mum never even woke me up at 6:00 a.m. All the other village girls would even get to the stream at 6:30 a.m. or so, and I would get there at 7:30 a.m. These people must think I'll play by the rules here, but not me," she said to herself, smirking.

Tutu was so happy to be there. She saw every challenge as an opportunity. Even though she wasn't used to waking up at 5:30 a.m. at home, she knew that this was an opportunity to do even more chores and achieve more in a day! At the end of the assembly, they each went to their hostels and retired for the night.

* * *

Early the next morning, at exactly 5:30 a.m., there was a loud sound. It was the morning bell. A lot of the young ladies grumbled because they weren't used to waking up that early. The School Warden came with a whistle. "You have only five minutes to put on your workout clothes and follow me," she said.

"Tomorrow you won't have this luxury, so it would be better if you go to bed in your jogging clothes! I'm being lenient today because you are all new here."

"Okay, run along now," she yelled, blowing her whistle after the five minutes were up.

Clara was still putting on her shoes. "What, didn't you hear me? You only had five minutes!"

"I don't wake up at this time in my home, why do I have to wake up this early? I don't like school, I never did!" Clara mumbled.

"Did I hear you say you don't like school? Schooling is for your own good. It makes you a better person and helps you attain heights that even your parents could not reach."

"I don't care about heights! All I care about is my sleep, thank you. And I don't need anyone telling me that I have to like school or telling me what to do," Clara said.

"You would do well to listen and obey," the School Warden replied. "This is a strict school, and there are rules and consequences."

"Or what? She asked rudely. Will you send me to detention? I would gladly prefer that to jogging!" Clara snorted.

The School Warden had heard enough. She gave her a detention slip and sent her to the detention ground.

* * *

At the detention ground, there was a male prefect waiting for her. "Oh, I see you're my first student today. You are welcome. It's the right time for a jog, don't you think?"

"I thought this was the detention ground. Why am I still going to jog?" Clara cried.

"Oh, it is, quite alright, but for any chore you refuse to do, you get double here. So since you were to jog two miles this morning, and you didn't go with the others, you get to jog four with me! Am I not a handsome partner?" he said with a big smile on his face.

"Well, I guess you are," Clara reluctantly admitted and started jogging with him. At the end of the four miles, she was panting so much she tried to catch her breath.

"You must be out of shape. You need to come here more often," the School Prefect told her.

"No thanks," she replied. And she hurried back to her hostel. She almost missed taking her shower as it was 6:30 a.m. now, and she should have started cleaning her surroundings. She took a quick bath and got back just in time to throw her blanket across her unmade bed.

* * *

The School Mistress and School Warden were carrying out the morning inspection of the students' beds and surroundings. Tutu's bed was the bunk above Clara's. As it got to Clara's turn, she was quivering because she knew she hadn't laid her bed. Tutu stepped in front of her and said Clara's bed was hers. The School Mistress looked at her and asked for her name. She told her, and the School Warden pointed out that the names didn't match. Unknown to them, their names had been written on the bunk and the name Clara was written on the bed that Tutu claimed was hers.

"Did you not sleep in the bed assigned to you, or are you covering up for your friend"? the School Mistress asked.

Tutu was speechless and could not say a word.

"Okay, for covering up for your friend, you'll go on detention," the School Warden said. She gave Tutu a detention slip and sent her off to detention. Clara was astonished. No one had ever stood up for her before, let alone served punishment for her. She watched with admiration as Tutu left the hostel.

"Listen and learn, everyone," said the mistress. "I will not have cover-ups. Everyone will serve whatever detention they get for their own disobedience. I hope you are all learning this lesson. By the way, at the end of the school year, there is going to be a competition of your handcraft and cooking. I hope at least one of you will make me proud."

Clara looked appalled. She hadn't learned any trade, let alone how to cook.

* * *

Meanwhile, Tutu was on her way to the detention ground. She met the male School Prefect and greeted him. "Good morning," she said in her sweet voice.

"Good morning," he replied. "Everyone who comes here is always so grouchy. How come you are so nice?" "Well, I guess, I'm not everyone," she replied. "I have a personality of my own, I am special."

"Oh, really, so why were you sent here? Let me see your detention slip."

She gave it to him, and he said, "Covering up for your friend? That's different Why would anyone go to detention for a friend?"

"She's actually not my friend. We only just met, but I saw how unfortunate it was that she missed out on our regular schedule, and she turned up almost late for the inspection and didn't have time to make her bed. I felt bad for her and So I said the bed was mine, and that's how I got my detention," she replied.

"Why was she late? Where was she?" he asked. "She was in detention," she muttered.

"Oh, that grouchy young lady; Okay, I see, she jogged four miles with me. So how many miles do you want to jog with me today?"

"That's up to you. You pick."

"Okay, as you wish. Since you were covering up for her and she jogged four miles, let's have you jog for five miles!"

She smiled. "Not a problem."

The School Prefect was astonished. Not only was she doing detention for someone who was just an acquaintance,

She was also jogging more miles. She really is a rare gem, he thought to himself.

Unknown to the students, this handsome, male School Prefect was the Prince! His father had told him he was to get a job for two years before he could marry his betrothed and take up the throne. And he had said to himself, "What better place to work than at my father's school!" He therefore took the job at the school as the detention master.

He found himself laughing at the jokes and comments Tutu made and, in turn, told jokes of his own. At the end of the five-mile jog, Tutu thanked him for a wonderful time and went her way.

Not only was she nice, but she was also polite, the Prince noted. He hoped he would see her again someday.

* * *

Tutu went to class without breakfast as she had missed it while she was still in detention. It was a cleaning lesson. The teacher showed them how to scrub the kitchen floor and let them each take turns trying. Clara got the least marks in the class and after a short time, she was fed up. "I'm hungry," she said. "I need my lunch."

"You aren't leaving this class until you get at least 50 percent in your cleaning test," the teacher said. At this time, it was 11:25 a.m.

The school bell rang at 11:30 a.m. for recess, and Tutu stayed behind to help Clara.

"Why are you being so nice to me? What are you trying to be, an angel?" Clara asked.

"No, I'm just happy to help someone in need," Tutu replied.

"Well, I don't need your help," Clara snorted. "You think you can just come here and take over everything, Miss Goody Two-shoes? I remember you. You are the girl who got the special gold coin at the village stream!"

"Shh," Tutu replied. "You don't have to shout it from the rooftops!"

"You think you're better than me. Well, I know your little game, and I can play it too. I'm not going to let you beat me at this one. I'm going to get that prize, now watch me!"

"What prize are you talking about?" Tutu asked, perplexed.

Rachel, one of the other girls, came into the classroom because she forgot her purse. "Oh, didn't you hear about the competition? There's going to be one at the end of the school year on handcraft and cooking. My dad is a potter; I'm going to ask him to teach me how to make those beautiful cups of his. I hope I win!" And with that, she took her purse and ran off.

"Yeah, that's right, but I'm the one who's going to win. My dad is a fisherman though. I wonder what craft I can bring," Clara said.

Tutu smiled to herself. Since weaving clothes was her specialty, she didn't need anyone to teach her, and she could be ready by the end of the school year!

Tutu went off to her break while Clara finished her chores. As she walked away, Clara decided to be as hardworking as Tutu in order to win the prize.

* * *

Chapter Five

TUTU AND THE PRINCE

The end of the school year was drawing near, and there was excitement in the air. The Prince would be at the ceremony to pick the winner of the competition! All the eligible ladies had, by this time, celebrated their eighteenth birthdays and were of the accepted marriageable age.

Word was out that the Prince was betrothed to some mystery Princess whom no one had ever seen.

Meanwhile, in the palace, there was a lot of activity going on in preparation for the Prince's engagement party. All this time, the Prince had been secretly falling for Tutu. He had bumped into her several times on the way to the school brook and they had chatted and laughed about their detention experience together. He wished his engagement wasn't so soon. He was hoping to catch a glimpse of Tutu every now and then on her way to class or on her morning jog.

* * *

One day, the king sent for his son.

"My son," he said, "you know the time has come for you to take your rightful place as the heir to the throne. It is time you meet your betrothed and show her to our people."

"That's just the problem, Dad," he said. "How can I love someone I haven't met? I know you told me about your quest for a wife for me, but I've fallen in love with someone else."

"What! That can't be! I told you I want you to marry the best. How is it that you have kept this from me and fallen in love with someone else?"

"Please, Dad, you have to understand that I usually agree to whatever you want, but in this matter, I have to choose. I promise you, you will not be disappointed."

The king was outraged! "How can you disobey my orders?" He sent for his chief adviser.

"Have you told the girl's parents that it is time for their engagement?" "Not yet, sir. I was waiting for your order," the chief adviser said.

"Then go now and tell them that it will be at sundown three market days from today. It will give them enough time to prepare."

"Please, Dad, that isn't enough time. I haven't even told the one I love!"

"That's very good because you will not be doing that! I have picked a wife fit for a Prince. I forbid you to go back to that job! Stay here in the palace and prepare for your wedding!"

"Dad, may I at least go to the competition that will be taking place tomorrow? I'm the guest of honor."

"Well, if you must," the king replied.

The Prince hurried back to the school. "Tutu," he cried when he saw her by the well, their favorite meeting place. "There's something I must tell you. I'm sorry I've been keeping it a secret all this time, but you have to know that—"

Just then the School Warden happened to pass by the well. "My lord, the Prince," she cried as she knelt down, "we weren't expecting you until tomorrow!"

The Prince! Tutu was shocked; the male Prefect was the Prince! What a way to find out. Tutu turned her back so he couldn't see how embarrassed she was.

"I'm so sorry you had to hear it this way," he said. "I wanted you to hear it from me directly." "Well, it doesn't matter now," Tutu replied "My lord, the Prince," and she curtsied.

He didn't want the conversation to take this turn, so he took her hand and said, "Tutu, I'm still your friend."

"How can I be your friend?" Tutu asked. "You are the Prince, and I'm a mere peasant. We have nothing in common. You know oil and water do not mix," she cried as she pulled away and ran toward her hostel.

* * *

The Prince was perplexed at the turn of events; he went back to his palace and could hardly sleep all night. He feigned sickness the next morning because he didn't want to go back to the school and meet Tutu in the state he had left her.

His servants cajoled him into going there after lunch, and he finally obliged.

At the competition, he was asked to choose the best handcraft that he liked and he did. It was a beautiful handwoven piece of cloth. As the evening drew to a close, he was asked to sample the delicacies that the ladies had made, and one caught his fancy so much he asked if he could dance with the lady who made it. The School Mistress called her out, and it happened to be Tutu.

"Did you call me out to taunt me?" Tutu asked

"No," the Prince replied. "I just wanted to dance with the lady who made this delicious meal. I'm still going to dance with the lady who wove this cloth."

He held up the piece of cloth she had woven.

"Well, I guess that would be me," she replied.

"You? You are a young woman of many talents. You truly are a rare gem. Will you do me the honor of being my wife?"

Tutu burst into tears. "I would love to marry you, but alas, I was betrothed to someone I have never met two years ago.

I'm sorry, I cannot marry you." And with that, she ran out of the hall.

The Prince was so sad he had to leave early even before the end of the event and said his good-byes in a hurry.

* * *

The next day, he went looking for Tutu again but was told that her parents had come to get her in preparation for her wedding.

He was so sad and thought all hope was lost. All he could do was daydream of the good times they had together. How can I ever love another? he wondered. Well, he wouldn't.

He refused to eat even though the queen came and implored him to. She didn't want the crown Prince to look haggard and thin on his engagement day.

As the day drew near, Tutu wondered who her husband would be. The chief adviser to the king was strongly warned not to let her parents know whom she was marrying. He only said it was an important lord who lived far away. As she had all the beautification rituals done, she wondered in her heart what it would be like to live with someone she did not love.

Tutu had always been an obedient girl, so it never crossed her mind to be disobedient. Clara came with two of her friends to see her a day before the engagement.

"I hear you are to be married to someone you have never met," she taunted. "It's just as well, Miss Goody Two-shoes, and I hope you end up miserable."

"Don't say that, Clara," Yemi said. "I wish I were the one getting married tomorrow even though it is to someone I don't know."

"I'd rather stay unmarried, if you ask me, until someone I love takes me to the altar," Rachel said.

"Well, no one asked you, so you better run along now, my dear. The bride needs her beauty sleep," Rachel's mother said as she helped to pack things up. She had been involved in the beautification rituals for the bride.

Tutu gratefully went to bed, wondering what tomorrow held in store for her.

At the crack of dawn, Tutu let out a sleepy yawn. She suddenly developed cold feet. "Mother, I can't go through with this. I have to tell my betrothed that I'm in love with someone else. Surely, there is a law that would allow me to marry the man I love and who is willing to marry me."

Her mother sadly said, "Well, my dear, that is for your betrothed to decide," as she put the finishing touches to her dress. "You will just have to hope that he understands."

As the king's servants came to escort Tutu to the palace, she wondered if a man like her betrothed would ever agree to release her from the engagement and allow her to marry the one she loved.

She saw the Prince come into the palace and wondered if he had been invited to the ceremony. He looks so unhappy, she thought.

The arrival of the king was announced, and she recognized him as the old pauper who sat by the road on the way to the village stream. This is interesting, she thought.

The king then asked his son to come forward and meet his bride.

"That's me," she thought and muttered to herself, and she stood up. So did the Prince who came forward and unveiled her face.

"You!" he exclaimed. "Tutu, YOU are my bride?"

Tutu was at a loss for words. She was enthralled! "I am your bride?" she stuttered.

The Prince was so happy that he swept her off her feet and gave her a kiss. "Daddy, meet my bride!" he exclaimed.

"You two have met?" the king said. "You have to tell me all about it." He looked at the queen. "I gave an order that they should not meet beforehand !"

"That's impossible," the queen said to Tutu and the Prince. "How is it possible that you two have met? I had them under strict surveillance the whole time!" The king demanded that the servants in charge be summoned. The servants were questioned, and they all claimed that it was impossible that the Prince had met Tutu.They knew nothing about it.

The king then addressed the Prince and Tutu, "How on earth did you two meet?" He was incredulous.

They looked into each other's eyes, smiled and replied "It's a long, beautiful story...

Materials Used for Celebrations:

Five tubers of yams – five pieces of large size whole yam

A keg of the local wine—A small barrel of local wine

A bowl of kola nut-A plant species of the family of MALVACEAE also refer to as Cola acuminata and Cola nitida

A bottle of organic honey

A bowl of bitter kola –*Garcinia Kola Heckel* – A plant species of the family of CLUSIACEAE, also known as wonder plant, is a large brown nut containing e.g. caffeine; it's a source of cola extract

Watch out for: Book II

Tutu: Adventure in the Forest of No Return